Jack's Talent

Maryann
Cocca-
Leffler

Farrar, Straus and Giroux • New York

Distributed in Canada by Douglas & McIntyre Ltd.
Color separations by Chroma Graphics PTE Ltd.
Printed and bound in the United States of America by Phoenix Color Corporation
Designed by Irene Metaxatos
First edition, 2007
1 3 5 7 9 10 8 6 4 2

www.fsgkidsbooks.com

Library of Congress Cataloging-in-Publication Data
Cocca-Leffler, Maryann, date.
    Jack's talent / Maryann Cocca-Leffler.— 1st ed.
        p.   cm.
    Summary: On the first day of school, as the children in Miss Lucinda's class introduce
themselves and name their special talent, Jack wonders if he is good at anything.
    ISBN-13: 978-0-374-33681-3
    ISBN-10: 0-374-33681-4
    [1. First day of school—Fiction.   2. Schools—Fiction.]   I. Title.

PZ7.C638 Jac 2007
[E]—dc22
                                                                    2006048951

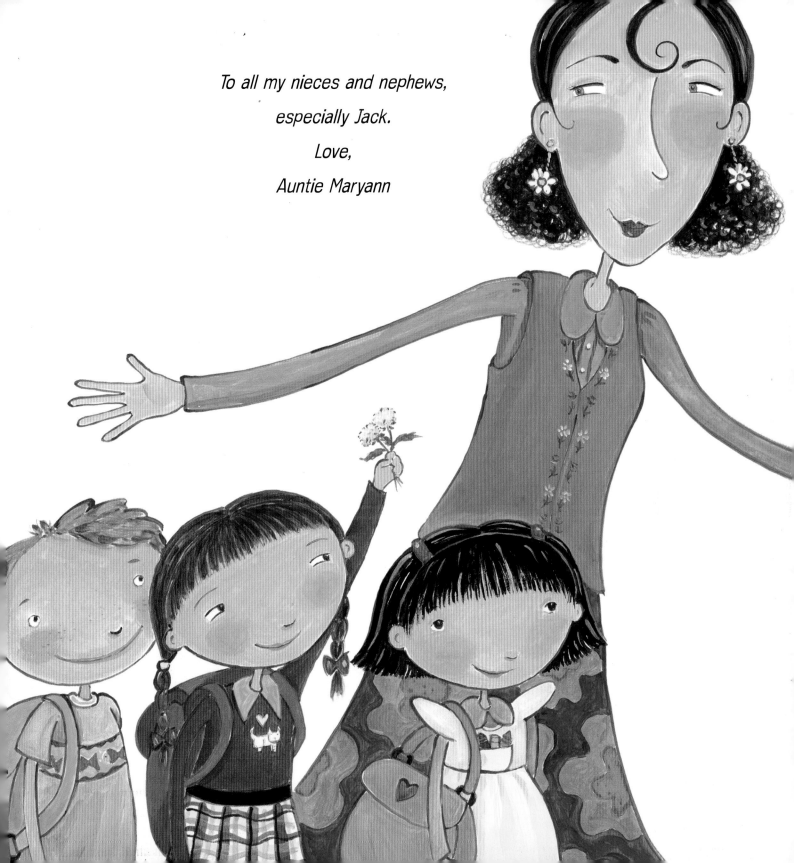

To all my nieces and nephews,
especially Jack.
Love,
Auntie Maryann

It was the first day of school.
Miss Lucinda gathered the children on the story rug.
"I will need to make name tags so I can remember you," she said.
"I want to learn everybody's name and special talent."

"What is a talent?" asked Jack.
"A talent is something that you are good at,"
said Miss Lucinda.

"I will start.
I am MISS LUCINDA.

I plant flowers and watch them grow.
I am good at gardening."

Michael went next.
"I am MICHAEL.

I can write long words.
I am good at spelling."

"I am FRANCESCA.

I can kick a ball really far.
I am good at soccer."

"I am MATTHEW.

When I go fishing with Grandpa,
I always catch the biggest fish.
I am good at fishing."

"I am OLIVIA.

I look for bugs. I found this one outside.
I am good at bug catching."

"I am CANDACE.

I make beautiful pictures of cats.
I am good at drawing."

"I am ALEX.

I can make giant sandcastles.
I am good at building."

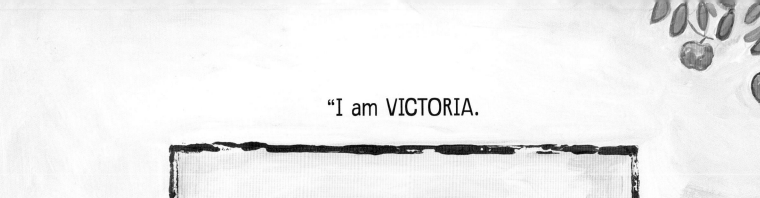

"I am VICTORIA.

I teach my dog, Cosmo, fancy tricks.
I am good at dog training."

"I am KRISTIN.

I perform for my friends.
I am good at singing."

Then it was Jack's turn.
Jack was quiet for a long time.

"I am JACK.
I am not good at anything."

"You must be good at something," said Miss Lucinda.

"Everyone has a special talent."

"Not me," said Jack.

"I am not good at spelling like MICHAEL.

I am not good at soccer like FRANCESCA.

I am not good at fishing like MATTHEW.

I am not good at bug catching like OLIVIA.

I am not good at drawing like CANDACE.

I am not good at building like ALEX.

I am not good at dog training like VICTORIA.

I am not good at singing like KRISTIN.

I am not good at anything."

"But you *are* good at something!" said Miss Lucinda.
"You are good at remembering,
and that is a *very* special talent.
I have an idea," she said.

"Jack, you may give out the name tags."

"I am JACK.

I am good at remembering."